# Picnic!

## A Day in the Park

From:
Mrs. Peña

# By Joan Holub
## Illustrated by Will Terry

SCHOLASTIC INC.
New York  Toronto  London  Auckland
Sydney  Mexico City  New Delhi  Hong Kong

For Dia Calhoun,
author and friend –J. H.

ISBN 978-0-545-24961-4

Text copyright © 2008 by Joan Holub.
Illustrations copyright © 2008 by Will Terry.
All rights reserved. Published by Scholastic Inc.,
557 Broadway, New York, NY 10012, by arrangement
with Aladdin Paperbacks, an imprint of Simon & Schuster
Children's Publishing Division, READY-TO-READ
is a registered trademark of Simon & Schuster, Inc.
SCHOLASTIC and associated logos are trademarks
and/or registered trademarks of Scholastic Inc.

12 11 10 9 8                    11 12 13 14 15/0

Printed in the U.S.A.                    40

First Scholastic printing, March 2010

Designed by Lisa Vega
The text of this book was set in font Century Oldstyle BT.

"This way!" called Jay.

"Corn cob," said Rob.

"Watermelon,"
said Helen.

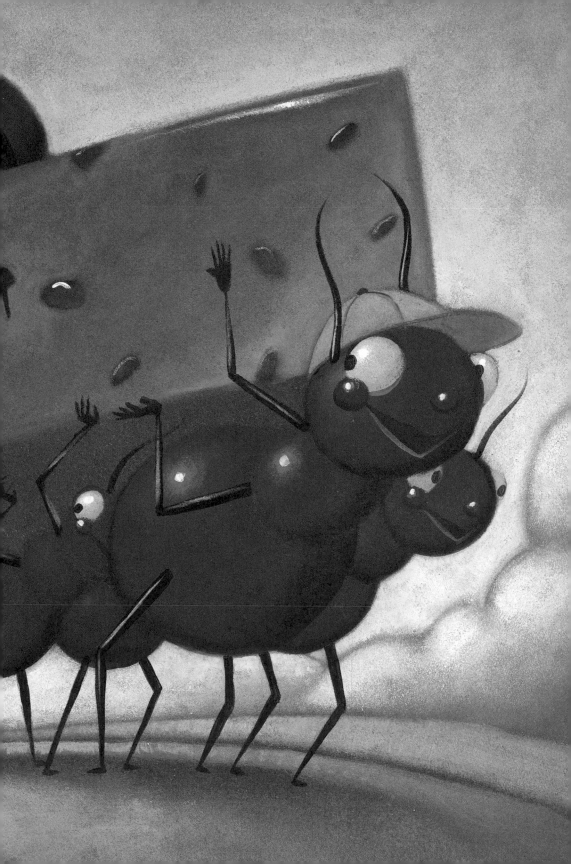

"A bean," said Jean.
"A pea," said Dee.

"A roll," said Noel.
"And jam," said Pam.

"And pie!" said Guy.

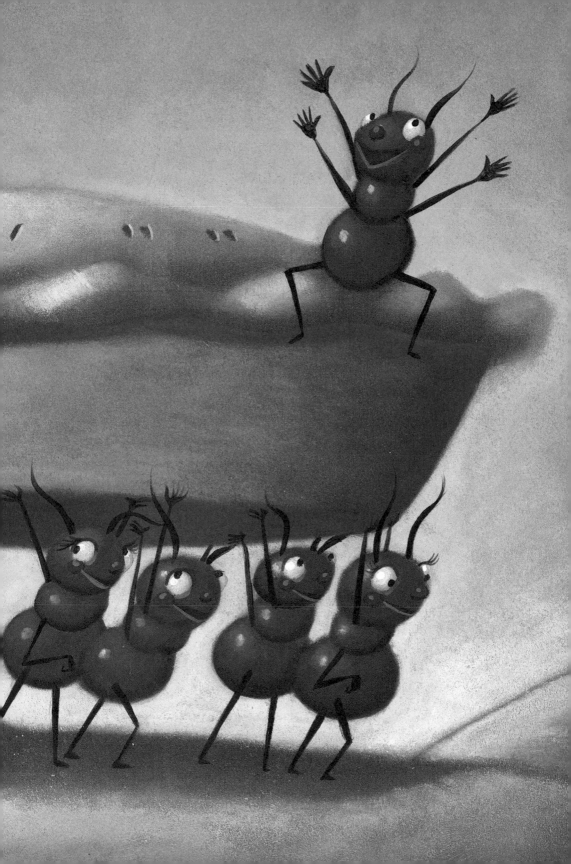

"Picnic," said Nick.

"All gone," said Dawn.

"Time to go," said Joe.

"Which way?" asked Jay.
"Don't know," said Joe.

"Can't see," said Dee.
"Too dark," said Clark.

*Blink, blink,*
went Link.

*Flash, flash,* went Nash.

"This way!"
said Jay.

"Thank you,"
called Drew.

"Good night," said Dwight.